For more than forty years,
Yearling has been the leading name
in classic and award-winning literature
for young readers.

Yearling books feature children's
favorite authors and characters,
providing dynamic stories of adventure,
humor, history, mystery, and fantasy.

Trust Yearling paperbacks to entertain,
inspire, and promote the love of reading
in all children.

Other Books About Calvin Coconut

TROUBLE MAGNET

DOG HEAVEN

ZOO BREATH

CALVIN COCONUT

THE
ZIPPY FIX

Graham Salisbury

illustrated by
Jacqueline Rogers

A YEARLING BOOK

This is a work of fiction. Names, characters, places, and incidents either are the product of the author's imagination or are used fictitiously. Any resemblance to actual persons, living or dead, events, or locales is entirely coincidental.

Text copyright © 2009 by Graham Salisbury
Illustrations copyright © 2009 by Jacqueline Rogers

All rights reserved. Published in the United States by Yearling, an imprint of Random House Children's Books, a division of Random House, Inc., New York. Originally published in hardcover in the United States by Wendy Lamb Books, an imprint of Random House Children's Books, a division of Random House, Inc., New York, in 2009.

Yearling and the jumping horse design are registered trademarks of Random House, Inc.

Visit us on the Web! www.randomhouse.com/kids
Educators and librarians, for a variety of teaching tools, visit us at www.randomhouse.com/teachers

The Library of Congress has cataloged the hardcover edition of this work as follows:
Salisbury, Graham.
Calvin Coconut : the Zippy fix / Graham Salisbury ; illustrated by Jacqueline Rogers.
p. cm.
Summary: Calvin tries to earn money to buy Stella, the babysitter, a present for her sixteenth birthday because he feels guilty for taking advantage of her allergy to cats.
ISBN 978-0-385-73702-9 (trade) – ISBN 978-0-385-90640-1 (lib. bdg.)
ISBN 978-0-375-89394-0 (e-book)
[1. Moneymaking projects–Fiction. 2. Family life–Fiction. 3. Hawaii–Fiction.]
I. Rogers, Jacqueline, ill. II. Title. III. Title: Zippy fix.
PZ7.S15225 Cae
[Fic]–dc22
2008036221

ISBN 978-0-375-84601-4 (pbk.)

Printed in the United States of America

10 9 8 7 6 5 4 3 2

First Yearling Edition

For Ace

Dream
Then make it happen
—G.S.

For Cessy with love
—J.R.

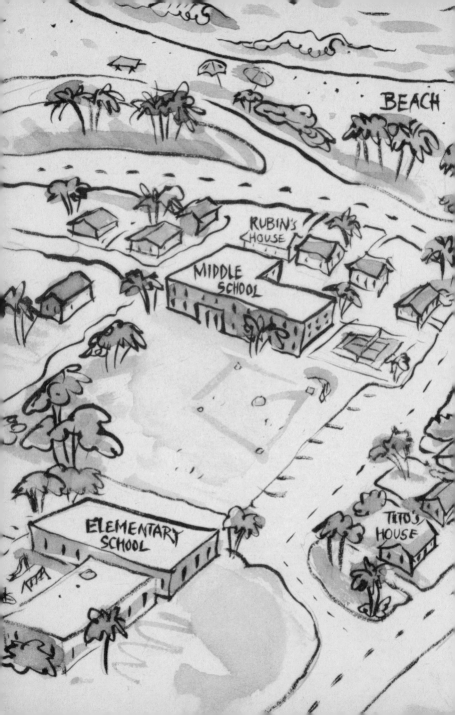

1

Rodents of Hawaii

Manly Stanley the centipede, our class pet, looked out at us from inside a jar on our teacher Mr. Purdy's desk. He was frowning and pounding fifty of his one hundred legs on the glass. I knew what he was thinking: why were we drawing pictures of things that would love to eat him?

Hey! he seemed to shout. What's going on out there? Let me see!

Julio, Rubin, Willy, and I were crowded around my desk working on a science poster. Our project was called Rodents of Hawaii.

We'd drawn pictures of a mouse, a rat, a guinea pig, and a gerbil. We wanted to put a hamster and a mongoose in there, too, but Mr. Purdy said hamsters were illegal in the islands. They could bring in diseases. And a mongoose is a carnivore, not a rodent.

We were stumped.

Manly Stanley raced up onto his rock and stretched his neck for a better look. "Hey, Manly," I said. "You know of any more rodents we can draw?"

Julio snorted. "He should. Rodents love centipedes."

Manly Stanley cringed and scurried down into the shadows.

"Look, Julio. You scared him."

"Pfff."

I tapped on the glass. "Don't worry, Manly, I'll protect you."

"Come on, guys," Rubin said. "We're wasting time."

I poked my chin with my black Sharpie. "Are moles rodents?"

"Yeah, moles!" Julio said.

"You got moles here?" Willy asked. He was from California and knew lots of stuff we didn't. "I haven't seen any."

"I got a mole in my armpit," Rubin said. "Want to see it?"

Willy laughed.

Me and Julio looked at Rubin like, Are you for real?

Rubin put up his hands. "I'm just saying."

Mr. Purdy walked by and glanced down at our poster. "Great work, boys. Keep going."

We looked up and grinned. "We will, Mr. Purdy. But we can't think of any more rodents."

Mr. Purdy pinched his jaw. "Well now. Let's see. Why don't you think of yourself as a cat? What rodents might you see if you were hunting in the weeds?"

"Yeah-yeah," Julio said. "Be a cat. That's good, Mr. Purdy, thanks."

Mr. Purdy winked and moved on.

Rubin bent close and mumbled, "Just don't be a black cat, or else we might get bad luck."

Julio scoffed. "Then I'm a black one, Rubin. Just for you."

"Black, yellow, green, or purple," I said. "Mr. Purdy had a good idea. So pretend you're a cat. What do you see?"

Rubin snapped his fingers. "A mouse."

"We already have a mouse," I said.

"We can have two."

Julio elbowed Rubin away from the table. "You're not *helping*, Rubin. Go breathe your dead squid breath on Shayla or something."

Mr. Purdy was leaning over Maya's desk, helping her. He looked at us over his shoulder.

Julio pointed at Rubin and started to say something.

I grabbed his arm. "Don't, Julio, you're going to get us in trouble."

Mr. Purdy gave us his raised-eyebrow look. He had been in the army and could really do that good, even better than Mrs.

5

Leonard, the principal. "Is there a problem over there, boys?"

I gave Mr. Purdy my best smile. "No, Mr. Purdy. No problem. Right, Julio?" I banged Julio's arm.

"Just kidding," Julio said, white teeth gleaming.

Mr. Purdy nodded and turned back to Maya.

Rubin leaned close and tapped the table with his finger. "See what I mean? You just mention black cats and you got trouble. You got to watch out. Believe it, or don't."

And I didn't.

Too bad . . . because Rubin was right.

2

zippy

After school I rode my bike home with Willy and Julio.

Usually I had to walk with my little sister, Darci. But she had a cough that morning and was over at Mrs. Nakashima's house while Mom was at work.

We rode straight up, with our arms hanging

loose at our sides. It was so hot even the my-nah birds were looking for shade.

When we cruised around the corner onto our street, I slammed on my brakes.

Julio nearly fell off his bike trying to keep from crashing into me.

Willy swerved and sailed into somebody's hedge.

"Why'd you stop?" Julio spat.

"Look."

I dipped my head toward Maya's cat, sprawled in the middle of the street.

Julio looked at me like, Are you nuts? "You caused a wreck because of Maya's *cat*?"

Willy yanked himself and his bike out of the hedge and studied the scratches on his arms.

"Sorry," I said.

Willy waved it off. "I'm okay."

Julio stared at me.

"What?" I said. "It's a black cat."

"It was black yesterday, too. And last month and last year. So what?"

"Well, Rubin said–"

Julio threw up his hands. "Not Rubin again."

"No, but . . . it's . . . well."

Willy held his front tire between his legs and straightened out his handlebars. "They *must* be bad luck. Look how we crashed."

"That was Calvin," Julio spat. "Not the cat!"

I chewed on my thumbnail and considered the furry black mass lying in the middle of the road. His name was Zippy, but zippy he wasn't. He was lazy as a slug. Not very smart, either, because any cat that lounges in the middle of the street is looking to get run over by a car.

"You're right," I said, trying to shake Rubin's warning out of my head. "It's just superstition."

We got back on our bikes and coasted toward Zippy, circling him twice. Zippy stretched, his claws flashing out like knife blades.

Julio stopped and studied Zippy. "You are the laziest cat I've ever seen in my life, no question."

I got off my bike and kicked down the stand. "Come on, Zip." I scooped him up. "You stay out here in the street, some car's going to flatten you."

Zippy purred in my arms. I bet he weighed like a hundred pounds. "You should be out in the jungle chasing down the rodents of Hawaii."

Zippy gave me a lazy blink.

I set him down in the shade of a plumeria tree in Maya's yard. The grass was warm and soft, way better than the street. "I just don't want to see you get squashed, okay?"

Zippy gave me dirty looks.

I laughed. "You're something, Zipster."

"Laters!" Julio called from the street, heading home.

Willy jumped on his bike. "Me too."

I waved and turned back to Zippy. "Don't you give me bad luck, now. I did this for your own good. You listening to me, Zip?"

I scratched under his chin and left when he started purring again. I had no idea what a bad listener Zippy was.

3

Boooom

Mom's car was in the garage when I coasted into our driveway standing on the pedals. I skidded to a stop, dumped my bike on the grass, and went inside.

"What's going on?" The screen door slapped behind me.

Mom and my little sister Darci were in the

living room digging into a shopping bag from Macy's, where Mom worked in the jewelry department.

Mom looked up, smiled, and laid a silky green dress over the back of the couch. "Hi, sweetie, how was school?"

"Fine, but why are you home?"

"Last time I checked, this is where I live."

"Yeah, but you're supposed to be at work and Darci's supposed to be at Mrs. Nakashima's."

"I decided to take the day off."

I looked at Darci. "I thought you were sick."

Darci gave me an excited grin. "We bought a dress for Stella." I guess shopping cured her.

Mom picked up the green dress. "Isn't this stunning, Cal?"

Stunning? A hurricane is stunning. An explosion is stunning. A car crash. "Yeah, sure. What's it for?"

"Stella."

"She doesn't have a dress?"

"It's a special dress. A boy asked her to a dance."

"No joke?"

Mom pinched my cheek and kissed my head. "No joke."

Stella was almost sixteen and lived with us. She'd come from Texas and had been here about a month. We took her in because Stella's mom was my mom's best friend in high school.

Also, a couple years ago, my dad, now known as Little Johnny Coconut, the kind-of-famous singer, had split from Mom and moved to the mainland, where he lives with his new wife. Now Mom had to work six days a week and she needed help. Stella was it.

Somewhere down the street I heard the deep, low thumping of a car stereo.

Boooom . . . boooom . . . boooom.

It was the slow, spooky kind you can hear a mile away.

"The dance is at the high school," Mom went on.

Boooom . . . boooom . . . boooom.

Growing louder. Coming closer.

"It's Friday night," Mom continued. "That's why Darci and I went shopping."

"What?"

"Are you listening to me, Calvin?"

The booming radio got louder and louder . . . then went silent.

Mom's eyes shifted.

Outside, an engine rumbled low.

Darci ran to the window.

A car door thumped shut.

4

Watermelon

"Stella's home!" Darci yelped.

I ran up behind her and caught a glimpse of the car just as it pulled away. It rumbled like an army tank and was so low to the ground it could scrape gum off the street. A fat black stripe ran down the middle, front to back, and the car was pink!

Pink?

Boooom . . . boooom . . . boooom.

Mom stretched to look over my shoulder, but the car was gone. "Did you see who brought her home?"

"Some guy in a pink car."

"Oooo," Darci said.

Stella passed by the window outside, heading to the front door, her books hugged close to her chest. As usual she wore shorts, a tight shirt, and rubber slippers. It was impossible to imagine her in a dress.

The screen door squeaked open.

Mom smiled. "Welcome home, Stella."

Stella glanced around the room. "What's wrong? Why are you all here? Did we get robbed?"

"No, no, everything's fine." Mom hurried over and took Stella's books from her. "Follow me. We have something for you."

Darci couldn't stand it. "Mom got you a dress! Mom got you a dress!" she said, bouncing on her toes.

Stella's face lit up. "A dress?"

"Look." Mom set the books down and picked up the green dress.

Stella's hand flew to her mouth, covering it, as if the dress was the most wonderful sight she'd ever seen.

Weird.

"Oh, Angela," Stella whispered.

Stella crept over, took the dress from Mom, and held it close. It fell to just above her knees. "You shouldn't have."

"Go try it on," Mom said.

Stella hurried into her bedroom. Which used to be mine. Which I had to give up when Stella moved in. Which sent me to a room made of half the garage. Which, actually, I liked better. Because who can live in a house with three girls?

Mom beamed, as pleased as I'd ever seen her.

Jeese, I thought. Maybe I should try that. Oh, Mom! This new T-shirt. You shouldn't have!

Naah.

Stella came back wearing the new dress and a huge grin. She twirled around. "Like it?"

Mom's eyes glossed. "Oh, Stella, you look so beautiful."

I gawked. I'd never seen Stella all dressed up. Her blond hair looked blonder. Her eyes twinkled like sequins. She even gave me a small smile. She was a totally different person.

Darci must have thought so, too, because all she could say was "Wow, wow, wow."

Mom put her arm over my shoulder and pulled me close. "What do you think, Cal? Doesn't she look fabulous?"

She looked pretty good, all right. The silky

smooth dress was the deep green color of a ripe watermelon. It somehow made Stella look like a nice person. "You look like . . . like . . . like a watermelon."

Darci spurted a laugh.

Mom covered her mouth, nearly laughing, too.

Stella's smile fell off her face. Her lips puckered and a squint shrank her eyes to olive pits.

What? Did I say something wrong?

Stella strode over and bent close, hands on her hips, her face inches from mine. "I look like a *what*?"

"Uh . . . a watermelon? You know, green?" What was the big deal?

"Well, you look like a tree stump."

I frowned. So I wasn't nine feet tall. So what?

Mom grabbed Stella by the shoulders and spun her around. "Let's go to my room and see if we can find just the right necklace to go with that dress. Oh my goodness, your mother would be *so proud* to see you now."

"No, she wouldn't," Stella whispered, and followed Mom down the hall.

I turned to Darci and spread my arms. "What'd I do?"

Darci grinned. "A watermelon?"

5

Stump

I absolutely did not have a problem following Rule Number Five on Mr. Purdy's list of fourth-grade boot camp rules: Be kind and respectful to others.

But when it came to Stella, it was really, really, *really* hard.

"Well, lookie, lookie," she said the next

morning when I stumbled into the kitchen. "Stump's up."

"Don't call me Stump," I mumbled, barely awake.

Stella was bagging Darci's school lunch. I put my hand up to shield my eyes from the bright sunlight streaming through the window.

"What's wrong with Stump?" Stella said. "It's a term of endearment, like Little Man or Peewee."

"Where's Mom?"

"A term of endearment is something nice you . . . you . . . *ah-choo!* . . . say about someone you like." She started to sneeze again but pinched her nose to stop it.

Something nice. Right.

I frowned and noticed her eyes were kind of puffy. I shrugged and took a bowl and a box of Rice Krispies and sat at the counter. "Watermelon," I mumbled to myself.

"Oh," Stella said, as if she'd just remembered something. "I dropped my hairbrush and it bounced under my bed, and I need

somebody really, really short to walk under there and get it for me, can you do that, honey? I'd be forever grateful."

"Hardy-har-har."

Stella sneezed again. "No, really, what's it like being a pygmy?"

"Mom! Stella's being mean to me!"

"I'm not being mean, honey. I'm just having some fun with you. Don't you know what fun is? It's when people are happy. They laugh and have a good time."

She pinched my cheek.

I jerked away. "Weirdo."

Stella smiled. "I feel good today."

"Why?"

"A stump would never understand."

"Don't call me *Stump*!"

"Stump. Peewee. Pygmy. Pip-squeak.

Squirt. Half-pint. Elfie. Runt. Shrimp. Shorty. Midget. Which one works for you?"

"Mom!"

"She can't hear you. She's getting ready for work."

I turned my back on Stella and reached into the cereal box for a handful of Rice Krispies. I was too tired to get the milk.

"Don't stick your filthy hands in there!" Stella snapped. "Other people eat Rice Krispies, too, you know."

Darci came blinking into the sunny kitchen and sat on the stool next to me. She was still in her pajamas. Pillow marks crisscrossed her cheek.

Stella slapped a bowl, a spoon, and a carton of milk in front of her. "Eat like a human being, not like your brother, the monkey."

Darci yawned and stretched. "Where's Mom?"

"Right here," Mom said, hurrying into the kitchen. "And as usual, I'm running late. Stella, will you . . . What happened to your eyes? Are your allergies acting up again?"

Stella sneezed. "No . . . I don't think so."

"Have you been around any cats?"

My ears perked up. Cats?

Stella shook her head.

Mom waved it off. "Your eyes are a little puffy, that's all. Anyway, will you see that Calvin and Darci leave for school in about ten minutes?"

"Sure."

Mom grabbed a brown-spotted banana and headed for the door. She stopped and looked

back. "So, Stella . . . I'm curious . . . what's his name?"

"Who?"

"The new guy?"

Yeah, I thought. What kind of name would a pink-car guy have?

Stella hesitated. " It's . . . Clarence."

Mom cocked her head. "Now, that's a name you don't hear too often."

"He's a senior."

"Well, I'm looking forward to meeting him." Mom blew us a kiss and left.

I turned to Stella. "Who's Clarence?"

"Who's short?"

All that day at school it was like a Stella chant running through my head: *Stump, Pygmy, Peewee. Stump, Pygmy, Peewee.* I had to stop this short stuff before it got out of hand and spread to school. I could almost hear big sixth-grade bully Tito Andrade and his friend Frankie Diamond shouting, "Hey, Coco-stump! Howzit?

Whatchoo say, Coco-short, can I use your head
for an armrest? Bwahahahaha!"

Dumb Stella. It just wasn't right.

And that night she kept on teasing me.

By the next morning I'd had enough.

So I did something about it.

6

Think Twice

It was hot and muggy that morning. No breeze. The ironwood trees across the street were completely still.

I went over to Julio's house, thinking maybe we'd grab Willy and go to the beach or something. It was Friday, but it was a Teachers' Day, so we had it off, even Stella.

I knocked on Julio's door.

As I waited for someone to answer I glanced down the street and saw Zippy wander out of Maya's garage. He stopped and looked toward me, as if to say, Hey.

I watched as he lumbered into the street for another hard day of trying to get murdered by a car.

I shook my head.

"S'up?" Julio yawned and swung the screen door open.

"He's out there again." I turned toward Zippy.

Julio humphed. "Still black, too."

"Yeah. Hey, you want to do something?"

"Sure. What?"

An idea was brewing. "You know how I picked Zippy up a couple days ago? And you know Stella and how I told you she's allergic to cats? Well, listen to this: yesterday she sneezed a lot and I think it's because of I had Zippy all over me. Her eyes got puffy, too. I mean, how else would they get puffy?"

"Somebody punched her out?"

"No, seriously, Julio. Cats make her sneeze."

Julio yawned. "This is so exciting I can't stand it, Calvin."

I bit my thumbnail. "Come out. I have an idea."

Julio let the screen door slap behind him as we headed down the street. Zippy looked up, blinking in the sun.

Julio snorted. "You should be called Sleepy, not Zippy."

I squatted. "How's it going, Fats?"

Zippy closed his eyes and stretched out his neck when I scratched under his chin.

I glanced over my shoulder. No one watching from Maya's front window. Nobody on the street.

Julio turned, too. "What you looking at?"

"I need to borrow Zippy."

"For what?"

"Sneezes." I slipped my hands under Zippy's belly and lifted. "Man, are you sure you didn't swallow a bowling ball?"

Zippy purred.

I whispered in his ear. "Got a job for you."

Julio shook his head and followed me to my house.

Mom, Darci, and Stella had gone shopping on the other side of the island. Mom was on a mission to find *just the right necklace* for Stella to wear with her new watermelon dress. I guess Mom didn't have one she could borrow in her jewelry box.

"What are we doing? Julio asked.

"Making Stella sneeze."

"Why?"

"Because she calls me names." He didn't
need to know *what* names, and I sure wasn't
going to tell him. Anyway, I was going
to fix this name-calling stuff
right now, and Zippy
was my fixer.

"You mean like Stump?"

"Shuddup, Julio!"

Julio cracked up.

I carried Zippy to Stella's bedroom door. It was closed. There was a sign on it: THINK TWICE.

I inched the door open.

7

Danger Zone

"Stella?"

Julio jumped back. "She's home?"

"No, but with her you can't be too careful."

The bed was made. There were no piles of clothes on the floor. Books stood perfectly straight on either side of her radio/CD player.

On the wall above her bed was a new

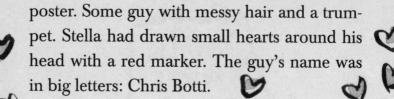

poster. Some guy with messy hair and a trumpet. Stella had drawn small hearts around his head with a red marker. The guy's name was in big letters: Chris Botti.

Julio pointed at a picture on her desk. "Who's this?"

From a silver frame, Stella's mom glowed like a movie star in an autographed black-and-white photo. *To Stella. Love, Twyla.*

Julio picked it up. "Twyla?"

"Her mom."

"Why'd she sign it *Twyla*? Why not *Mom*?"

I shrugged and set Zippy on the floor. "Her mom used to be an actress or something."

Julio snorted. "She looks like somebody in a magazine, not a mom."

"Maybe that's why she signed it *Twyla*."

Zippy sniffed the air and strutted over to the closet. A fat roach scurried out. Zippy shrank back and headed for the bed.

"You don't like those things, either, huh?"

The roach ran back into the closet. I figured he was relieved Zippy didn't mistake him

for a snack. I'd have to come back and catch him for Manly Stanley.

Zippy leaped up onto Stella's bed and settled down on her pillow. "Sure beats the road, doesn't it, Zipster?"

Zippy blinked.

"That might make her sneeze, all right," Julio said. "If she's allergic to cats."

"She is."

I felt a tiny pinch of guilt. Being in Stella's room with a cat was not only wrong, it was dangerous. If Stella caught me she'd smash me like a spider.

But she'd called me Stump! A million times. Anyway, a couple of sneezes was no big deal.

"Knock yourself out, Zip."

Me and Julio went into the kitchen for a snack.

When we came back, Zippy was snoring.

A soft, crunchy noise outside made me jump. It sounded like somebody creeping up to the window.

My heart nearly stopped.

Julio crouched and whispered, "What was *that*?"

It could have been anything. Somebody's dog nosing around the yard, a mongoose, a sudden breeze.

It could have been Stella, too. We had to get out of there.

I hefted Zippy off Stella's pillow. "Vacation's over, Fats."

Outside, I shooed him into the bushes. "Go find a mouse on your way home."

The guilt I'd felt in Stella's room was fading fast. And justice had been served.

I clapped Julio on the back. "I feel good."

"For sure, Calvin. You are one strange bazooks."

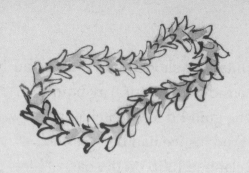

8

Crummy All Over

Julio and I wove through the trees, past our fort, and out onto the golf course. There was nothing going on, no golfers, and no jeep guys, who lived to run kids like us off the fairways.

So we went down to the river and threw rocks at fish.

After that, we searched for golf balls in the

swamp grass, where bad golfers tried to hit over the water.

"Gotta go," Julio finally said. "All this excitement is wearing me out."

"Yeah, me too."

When I got home, Mom and Darci were in the kitchen.

"There you are," Mom said. "What've you been up to?"

"Not much. Robbed a few stores, couple of banks."

"That's good. Darci, why don't you show Calvin what we got him."

"You got me something?"

"Stella picked it out."

"Stella? You're kidding."

Darci pulled a book out of a bag and handed it to me.

Mom tapped it with her finger. "You need to read more, Cal. I asked Stella to find you something that would hold your interest."

I studied the book.

Hatchet.

Cool title. It had a good cover.

"Stella read this in fifth grade and couldn't put it down. She thought you'd like it, too."

"She did?"

"Ask her yourself, except right now she's taking a nap. She has a date tonight."

"Clarence," Darci added.

Oh yeah, pink-car guy.

"Just wait till you see her all done up, Cal. She's gorgeous."

An hour before Clarence came to pick her up, Stella stumbled out of her room. Her eyes were like giant pink marshmallows with slits in them. Her face was splattered with red blotches. Her voice was dry and raspy. She looked like she'd just staggered out of Death Valley.

"Oh, no!" Mom gasped. "Stella, what happened?"

I gaped.

"Aller . . . gic . . . something . . ."

Tears squirted out of the slits.

I stopped breathing. Darci hid behind Mom.

"What *was* it?" Mom asked.

"Cat . . . I'm only . . . allergic . . . to cats."

Stella started sobbing. Mom put her arm around her and led her to the couch. "I'll call a doctor."

Stella shook her head. "No, please . . . it will go . . . away."

"But your *date*," Mom said.

I gulped.

Stella bolted up and ran to her room.

"That is just so sad," Mom said.

Darci looked scared. "Will Stella be all right, Mom?"

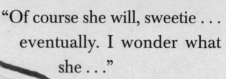

"Of course she will, sweetie . . . eventually. I wonder what she . . ."

Mom turned to me. "There couldn't have been any cats in this house, right, Cal?"

I shrugged. I couldn't speak. I felt like I'd just swallowed a fish hook and Mom was reeling me in.

At seven, Clarence came down the street for Stella.

Boooom . . . boooom . . . boooom.

Mom had wanted to call him and explain what had happened, but she didn't know his number, and Stella wasn't talking to anyone.

The booming radio went off. Seconds later Clarence was filling every inch of our screen door.

"Oh, dear," Mom said.

Darci and I followed her to the door, where we got our first real look at Clarence.

Ho, man!

He had wild Samoan hair and a line of tattoos on his dark, muscular neck. His sky blue silk shirt fell down over perfectly creased tan pants that bunched over brown leather shoes. A white ginger lei hung from his huge hand.

"I'm Clarence," he said. "Stella home?"

I winced.

"I'm so sorry, Clarence," Mom said. "Stella came down with something and . . . she can't go out tonight. She feels terrible about it."

Clarence glanced at Darci and me, peeking around Mom. Was it my imagination, or did he look at me longer? Could he know what I did to Stella? No . . . impossible.

But *could* he?

I shrank back.

Clarence turned back to Mom. "Oh," he said in a soft, understanding voice. "I'm sorry she feeling bad. No problem. I call tomorrow, see how she doing. Will you give Stella the lei?"

"Of course I will," Mom said, taking it. "How lovely!"

My stomach nearly barfed itself up.

All I'd wanted was to make her sneeze.

I felt crummy.

Crummy all over.

9

MAGNANIMOUS

"Monday is Stella's birthday," Mom said the next morning. "We've got to find a way to cheer that poor girl up, Calvin. After last night . . ."

Mom shook her head.

I was sitting at the kitchen counter with a bowl of cereal. Just out the window, Mrs. Nakashima's fence was a thick tangle of red bougainvillea. As always on a Saturday morning, Mom was zooming around getting ready to go to work.

No matter how hard I tried, I was unable to get Stella's swollen face out of my mind. It had cleared up some, but Stella had missed out on her big night.

I cringed thinking about how hard Mom and Darci had worked to help her look just right.

And I'd messed it all up.

The freaky thing was, I'd totally gotten away with it. I could step up and explain the whole thing in a heartbeat. But I didn't have the guts. I stayed in the shadows, like the roach in Stella's closet.

"She turns sixteen on Monday," Mom went on.

I nodded.

"Cal...I know you and Stella haven't hit it off yet, but birthdays are a time to set differences aside and celebrate. Know what I mean?"

"Yeah . . . sure."

I was thinking about Clarence. He'd called earlier, but Stella wouldn't talk to him because her voice was still squeaky. When Mom asked me again if I could think of any animals that might have gotten into the house, I said I bet it was a mouse.

"Are you listening to me, Calvin?"

I looked up. "Huh?"

Mom put her hand on my shoulder. "On Monday we're going to have a little party for her. I'm going to bring a cake home for after dinner."

"Oh."

I started to take a bite of cereal.

Mom bent close and whispered, "I think Stella would just love it if you made something nice to give her."

Milk dripped off my spoon.

Mom squeezed my shoulder. "There's plenty of time for you to think of something."

I gulped down the rest of my cereal. I was itchy to get out of the house. I didn't want to talk about Stella's birthday, and I sure didn't want to be around when she got up.

"I'm going over to Julio's."

Mom raised her hand to stop me. "Look, if you don't do anything else, at least make her a birthday card. Will you do that?"

My guilty conscience was giving me a headache. How could I fix what I'd done to Stella?

"Yeah, sure, Mom."

"I really think you should think of a gift, though. Celebrate. Be magnanimous."

"Huh?"

Mom smiled. "It means be more giving, Cal."

"But she calls me Stum—"

Mom put her finger on my lips and gave me her I-want-to-be-proud-of-you look. "I know you'll think of something. . . . Oh, before you go, will you wake Stella up? I have to leave."

Mom kissed my forehead and left.

Dang.

I crept down the hall to the sign on Stella's door.

THINK TWICE.

I thought twice . . . about being somewhere else.

I *really* didn't want to go in that room again. I turned the knob and peeked in. Stella was asleep, facing the wall. Her hair

covered her face and she was hugging her pillow.

"Stella?"

She didn't move.

I crept closer. Her sheet was pushed down around her feet. She slept in a T-shirt and light blue men's boxer shorts.

I looked up and studied the new poster above where she slept. Who's Chris Botti?

I shrugged and edged closer. Just wake her and run.

"Stella."

Still nothing.

"Stella," I said louder. "Mom's going to work. You have to get up."

When she still didn't move, I poked her shoulder with my finger. "Stella!"

She groaned and mumbled something I couldn't understand.

"You have to get up. Mom said."

She didn't move, but this time she whispered something even a rock could understand. "Get. Out. Of. My. Room."

"But Mom said—"

Stella sprang up and glared at me.

I staggered back.

"If you're not out of here in one second I'm going to reach down your throat and tear your heart out!"

Good enough for me.

10

The Jazz Musician

Outside, the grass was warm under my bare feet. Down the way at the curve in the road, Julio's house glistened bright white in the sun. Maybe he was up.

He was, but he'd gone somewhere with his dad.

So I went to Willy's.

"Hey," Willy said when I knocked on his door. He was eating toast. Purple jam stained one corner of his mouth.

Of all of us on our street, Willy was the only haole, a blond white boy. Julio was German-Filipino-Portuguese. Maya was pure Chinese, adopted from China, and I was a pot of stew: Italian-Filipino-Hawaiian-Chinese.

Willy held the door open. "Come on in."

Willy's dog came thumping up, wagging his tail. He nudged me with his fat head. "Hey, Bosco." I wished I had a dog. But Mom wouldn't let me. "They're so stinky," she'd said. "And they shed."

Bosco picked up a stuffed groundhog and followed us into the kitchen. It squeaked as he chewed on it.

Willy's mom and dad were reading the paper at

the kitchen table. "Good morning, Calvin," Mrs. Wolf said. "What are you doing out so early today?"

I shrugged. "Mom just went to work."

"Ah, yes . . . Macy's, right?"

"And I'm supposed to think of something to give Stella for her birthday," I blurted. No matter how I tried, I couldn't get what I'd done to Stella out of my mind.

Mrs. Wolf snapped her fingers. "Oh, Stella! From Texas."

"Yep."

"Surprise her," Mrs. Wolf said. "Girls love to be surprised."

"They do? How?"

"Well, what kinds of things does she like?"

She likes to call me Stump. She likes to chase me with a rolled-up magazine. She likes to mess up the bathroom with all her junk. She likes guys with trumpets and pink cars that make a lot of noise. "Well," I said, "she has a poster that she drew hearts on."

"Oh? What kind of poster?"

"Some guy's on it." I tried to remember. "Chris something . . . Body? No, Bot-tee . . . Chris Bo-tee."

"The jazz musician?"

"He had a trumpet."

"That's him," Mrs. Wolf said. "Chris Botti. Stella has excellent taste in music. I have every CD he's made."

"You do?" Willy asked.

"Sure. Stella must be a bit of a romantic. Chris Botti's version of 'When I Fall in Love' is the most beautiful I've ever heard."

I looked at Willy. Willy opened his hands.

"That's what you should get her, Calvin," she said. "Chris Botti's brand-new CD. It just came out this week. Here, I'll show it to you."

Mrs. Wolf grabbed the CD from a stack in a cabinet and handed it to me. It was the guy in the poster, all right.

"This would be a *very* nice gift, Calvin."

Well . . . if it just came out she wouldn't have it yet. And there were those hearts. "Good idea." I handed it back. "Thanks."

I followed Willy outside to shoot some hoops in his driveway. I dribbled the ball. Should I tell him about what Julio and I did with the Zipster?

No, no, no. Forget it. All of it. It never should have happened.

But I couldn't forget.

"Take a shot," Willy said.

Clank!

I couldn't hit anything. My guilty conscience was giving me a lecture: Do something nice for Stella. Get her that new CD, and maybe– *maybe*–the crummy feeling might go away.

I tossed the ball to Willy. "You want to walk into town?"

"What for?"

"See how much that Chris Botti CD costs."

11

Running Out of Time

"Sure, we have it," the guy at the music store said. "Just came in this week."

His nametag said KEONI. He had short spiky hair and two gold rings on the right side of his lower lip. Ouch. I sure wouldn't want rings poking through my lip.

He nodded toward the jazz section. "Look under *B*."

Willy found it. "Here he is."

"Ho! He has a lot of CDs."

"That's prob'ly because he's good."

I turned the CD over to see the price. "Ai-yai-*yai*!"

Willy grabbed it. "Eighteen dollars! You got that much?"

I pulled out a crumpled one-dollar bill.

"Just one?"

I shrugged. "And thirty-one cents . . . in my bank . . . at home."

I jumped when Keoni came up behind us. "That's the new CD."

"Uh . . . yeah," I said. "Is it *really* eighteen dollars?"

Keoni grinned. "Yeah, really." He looked over his shoulder. "You like a few songs on it?" he whispered. "Download them on your computer. Save some money."

That would be good, but downloading was

out. Stella didn't have a computer, but she was saving for one.

I stuck Chris Botti back in the rack. The most money I'd ever had in my whole entire life was the ten-dollar bill I got for Christmas from Tutu Bunny, Mom's mom, who lived on Kauai. But that money was long gone.

"We have cheaper CDs," Keoni said. "There's a sale rack."

I frowned. "I just wanted this one."

Keoni shrugged. "Sorry."

Me and Willy left.

"With a dollar you can get her peanut M&M's," Willy said.

I considered that. "Or gum. She smacks it like firecrackers. Mom says it's not ladylike."

Calling me names wasn't ladylike, either, I wanted to add. But I kept that to myself. I didn't want Willy to know she called me Stump. I prayed Julio would keep his big fat mouth shut about it, too.

"Too bad about that CD," Willy said.

"It was a lot."

"Too much."

But the Chris Botti CD would *really* be something she'd like. And if eighteen dollars would make the crummy feeling go away it would be worth every penny.

I started walking faster.

Willy jogged to catch up. "What's the hurry?"

"I'm running out of time. Stella's birthday is Monday and I'm seventeen dollars short."

12

Cans

"You got any cans?" Willy asked as we hurried home.

"Cans?"

"Pop cans. Like what strawberry soda comes in, or root beer. You can recycle them and get money."

I slid to a stop and clapped my hand on his

shoulder. "Willy-my-man, you're a genius! We can collect cans!"

"Uh . . . I was just thinking maybe you had some in your house and you could . . . you know, turn them in."

"Right. And then we go to your house, and Julio's, and—"

"I get it," Willy said.

I flicked my eyebrows. "Let's do it."

At home I found nine empty Diet Sprite cans under the bottom shelf in the kitchen pantry. I grabbed a paper grocery bag and started tossing them in.

Two long feelers came waggling out of one of them. A huge, ugly brown cock-a-roach body followed them out.

"*Yah!*" I yelped, and dropped the can, which bounced on the tile floor and sent the roach flying. It landed on its back and struggled to turn over, legs wheeling.

"Man!" Willy gasped. "It's big as a mouse!" We backed off.

I got a butter knife out of the silverware drawer and flipped the roach over and waited for it to lug itself into the dark place under the shelf. Mom always stomped on them with her rubber slippers. But I hated to see the white guts come out.

I stuck the knife blade into the can's drinking hole and dropped the can into the grocery bag with the others.

"What are you twerps doing?"

Willy and I looked back over our shoulders.

Stella glared down on us. From that angle she seemed ten feet tall.

"Uhh," I sputtered. "We . . . uh . . . we're just, uh, taking these cans to . . . to . . . to make . . . a fort . . . yeah, a fort . . . for Willy's . . . uh . . . for Willy's army men."

Willy looked at me.

"A big fort," I added, seeing the story now. "He has these little rubber army guys, hundreds of them, thousands, maybe, and we're going to set them up and knock them down with . . . with . . . with rubber bands."

"And gravel," Willy said, catching on.

"And marbles."

I grinned at Stella.

Her face was as expressionless as a pancake. "You are so pathetic . . . both of you. And weird, too. How can you even live with yourselves?"

She grabbed a Diet Sprite and left the kitchen.

Willy turned to me. "Little rubber army guys?"

"I had to think of something."

"Actually, I do have a box of them."

"How about cans?"

We headed down to Willy's house with nine aluminum cans clacking together in the paper grocery bag.

Ahead, the black blob was lying out in the middle of the road again. A car turned onto our street and hit the brakes. The driver honked, but all Zippy did was raise his head as if to say, Can we get a little quiet here? Jeese.

The car drove around him.

Willy laughed. "Hey, there's Maya."

She was sitting on her skateboard in her front yard. Mayleen, Maya's older sister, was sitting on her heels behind Maya, braiding her hair.

I gave the cans to Willy and grabbed Zippy off the street.

"What's going on?" Maya asked.

I set the Zipster on the grass. "How come you don't care if Zippy's always in the street?"

Maya shrugged. "He does what he does. You can handcuff him to the mailbox if you want."

Zippy stood motionless, staring at nothing. That cat was in a class by himself. Maya blocked the sun with her hand. "Hi, Willy."

Willy hesitated. "Uh . . ."

"Well, anyway," I said, "we're collecting cans. Got any we can have?"

"Go ask my mom. She's cleaning out the car."

We found Mrs. Medeiros with her legs sticking out the open car door. We waited until she wiggled herself back out, her hands full of car junk.

Including a crushed pop can.

Mrs. Medeiros smiled when she saw us. "Well, hello, Calvin and Willy. What are you two up to?"

I shrugged. "Nothing. Can I have that pop can, Mrs. Medeiros? I'm collecting them."

"Sure." She handed it to me.

"You got any more we can have?"

Mrs. Medeiros threw the junk away and wiped her forehead with the back of her hand. "Inside. Let's go look."

Me and Willy walked away from Maya's house with eighteen new pop cans.

"Bye, Willy," Maya called.

I whispered, "She likes you."

Willy shoved me. "Shuddup!"

I staggered, laughing.

Surprising Stella was actually kind of fun. The crummy feeling was still there, but it was shrinking.

13

Pathetic

We got thirteen ginger ale cans at Mrs. Nakashima's house and seventeen Diet Coke cans at Willy's. Now we had so many we had to get a couple more grocery bags.

We went out to the patio and sat at a table with a shady umbrella in the middle. The grass in Willy's backyard was freshly mowed. It smelled good.

We dumped the cans onto the table and counted them.

Fifty-seven!

"What's fifty-seven times five cents?"

"Wait." Willy ran into the house and came back with a pencil and a piece of paper. "Okay . . . let's figure it out . . . oh, and here's four quarters I had in my room."

"But–"

"It's a loan. Don't worry about it."

"Fine, a loan." I grabbed the pencil. "So, fifty-seven times five."

Willy hunched close. "How much is it?"

I frowned at my calculation. Making money was *not* easy, especially when you're running out of time. "Three dollars and eighty-five cents, including your four quarters."

"That's it?"

I nodded. It was as depressing as two pages of word problems.

"Stella was right," I said. "We're pathetic."

14

Junior Criminal

We were getting tired of carrying three bags of pop cans around, so we decided to head over to Kalapawai Market and turn them into cash.

On the way we saw Maya skateboarding in the street, cool and easy, like a good surfer. She saw us and zoomed over. "Looks like you got a few more cans," she said, kicking her skateboard up into her hands.

"Fifty-seven."

"Why you collecting them, anyway?"

"Make money. I need to buy Stella a birthday present."

"I thought you didn't like her."

I shrugged.

"I heard she calls you Stump."

I squinted. "Who told you that?"

"Darci."

The little brat.

"I don't know what she's talking about. Come," I said, wanting to change the subject. "We're going to Kalapawai to cash them in."

Maya dropped her skateboard. "Boring." She zipped off, curving and ducking and standing with her back swayed like a surfer on the cover of a magazine.

"She's good," Willy said.

"Yep."

Kalapawai Market was a green and white

wood building that had been there since forever. They sold hats, maps, T-shirts, snacks,
newspapers, groceries, postcards, ice cream,
dried squid, cuttlefish, beach chairs, and anything else you needed.

Plus they gave you cash for your pop cans.

I stopped to recount what we had one last
time. "Still fifty-seven. And a few ants. But no
cock-a-roaches."

Willy grinned. "*Man*, that thing was big."

"Your cousin."

"Shuddup!"

Boy, did I feel good. I was with Willy and
we were about to get rich. The day just kept
getting better and better.

"Heyy," somebody said. "Coco-dork . . . what's in the bags?"

I turned to look.

Aw, man.

Tito Sinbad Andrade strolled up, smiling, almost like he was a nice guy. His hair hung in his eyes, making him look mysterious. But the only mystery you had to think about was if he was going to rob you or the guy next to you.

Tito pointed with his chin. "The bags,

Coco-my-man," he said with a wink. "What's in them?"

Frankie Diamond was with him. He stood behind Tito with his arms crossed. And behind Frankie was a guy named Bozo, who was just plain weird. They were sixth graders at our school, Kailua Elementary.

Frankie Diamond studied me, a half grin lifting one side of his mouth. Unlike Tito and Bozo, Frankie's T-shirt was clean, and his hair was slicked and shiny black. Around his neck, a silver chain glinted in the sun.

Tito stepped closer and peeked into one of the bags. "Ah," he said.

Bozo's eyes darted around like flies. "What they got, Tito? What they got?"

"Cans."

Bozo snorted. "Cans?"

Tito put a hand on my shoulder and pulled me close. "Listen . . . Coconut." He spoke pleasantly, softly. "I was coming here to buy me a big bag of sunflower seeds, but you know what? I'm sad, because . . . well, I no more nuff money . . . you see?"

Tito made an unhappy face. He opened his hands and looked down. "I need fifty cents more."

He shook his head. So sad.

With Tito, the smartest thing you can do is keep your mouth shut.

Tito snapped his fingers. "I got an idea! You can borrow me the fifty cents. Yeah! You can be my bank. Then I can get me that bag of sunflower seeds. How's about that . . . Coco-bank?"

Willy was as quiet as an ant.

Coming up behind me I heard *boooom* . . . *boooom* . . . *boooom*.

Coming closer.

I turned as a car pulled in and parked.

A pink car.

I'm saved!

15

Birfday

The booming radio went off.

"Ho," Tito said. "Check out that car! Sweet!"

Clarence got out. He towered over all of us.

When he glanced my way, I tipped my head toward Tito, hoping Clarence remembered me and would catch my silent message: He's robbing me!

Clarence raised an eyebrow and went into the store.

Dang.

Tito cocked his head. "You know him?"

"Kind of. And I'm not a bank."

"Sure you are," Tito said, forgetting about Clarence. "Look in those bags. You're rich." He tapped his chin with his finger. "Let's see, fifty cents would be . . . how many cans, Bozo?"

"Uh . . ." Bozo's lips moved as he counted on his fingers.

"Ten," Frankie Diamond said.

Tito grinned at me. "Frankie's good at math . . . so, how's about you borrow me ten of those cans, Coco-buddy? You got more than you need, ah?"

"I need them all, for a birthday pres—uh, I mean . . . I need them for . . . for . . ."

"A birfday present?" Tito grinned. "You

kidding, right? You don't give cans for a present."

"I just need them, that's all. I can't give you any."

"Thanks," Tito said, smiling big. He tapped my shoulder and snapped one of the bags out of my hand. "It's good to have friends like you."

I watched as Tito stole ten cans. When he was done, he looked up, surprised. "Ho! Had seventeen cans in this bag. That means you get to keep seven. Maybe your name is Coco-lucky."

Tito handed me the half-empty bag, winked, and headed into the store. "Have a nice day."

Bozo bumped me with his shoulder as he passed. "You should take them all, Tito. This punk don't need it."

"Be nice, Bozo. I'm a generous person."

Clarence passed them, coming out with a bag of sunflower seeds of his own. I wondered if he was taking them to Stella. He got in his car, started it up, and rumbled slowly away.

"Hoo-ie," Tito whispered, turning to watch him go. "I love that pink and black car."

Bozo tapped Tito's shoulder. "Man, you are good, Tito. You could sell ice cubes to camels."

"What?"

Bozo stopped to think. "No wait, you could sell ice cubes to ... to ..."

Frankie Diamond shoved Bozo through the door. "Eskimos, Bozo, Eskimos."

I felt sick. I'd just been robbed. It wasn't right.

Willy put his hand on my shoulder. "We'll find more."

We waited in the parking lot until Tito, Bozo, and Frankie Diamond came out and headed toward the beach.

They didn't even look at us. As far as they were concerned, we didn't exist.

I elbowed Willy. "Let's go cash these cans in before they come back."

We came out $2.35 richer. But we should have been $2.85 richer.

We sat in the shade at an outdoor table on the side of the store. "How much you have now?" Willy asked. "I mean if you add it to your money and my quarters?"

I grabbed a greasy paper plate out of a trash can and went into the store to borrow a pencil. I scratched it out. "Four dollars and sixty-six cents."

Willy brushed a fly off the table. "Someday somebody's going to rob Tito. When they do, I want to be there to see it."

"Me too."

Four small doves hopped around on the table next to us, hoping we might toss them some crumbs.

I slapped the table and stood. The birds

took off. "Just because I got robbed doesn't mean I'm giving up."

Willy followed me out into the sun.

"Where we going now?"

"Make more money."

"How?"

"I don't know, but I know who to ask."

"Who?"

"Uncle Scoop."

16

Shave Ice

Uncle Scoop's Lucky Lunch truck was parked under an ironwood tree facing the beach. Behind it families with squirmy babies and wild kids sat on blankets on the grass. Hamburgers and teriyaki sticks sizzled on small hibachis, and across the way, the ocean sparkled in the sun.

Uncle Scoop saw us coming. "Heyyy, how you kids doing?"

"Good, Uncle Scoop."

"I bet you came to cash in those coupons, right?" Uncle Scoop had given free shave ice coupons to me, Julio, and Willy after we got into trouble at school. But that's another story.

"I gave mine to my sister," I said.

Willy shook his head. "Mine's at home."

Uncle Scoop laughed. "I give you anyway. What you like? Red? Orange? Blue?"

"Thanks, Uncle Scoop," I said. "But do you know how I can make some money? I mean, by working . . . or something?"

"Money, huh? Well, let's see."

Uncle Scoop rubbed his chin. "You could ask your neighbors if you could mow their lawn."

"Yeah, but . . . I have to make it quick. Like, today, and anyway, our lawn mower won't start."

"Hmm, let's see." He crossed his arms, thinking. "I tell you what. Going be a big rush

88

soon . . . lunchtime . . . all those starving swimmers who forgot to bring their lunches will be coming over here any minute now, and I might need some help. You two ever make a shave ice?"

I looked at Willy, who shrugged.

"Guess not," I said.

"Never mind." Uncle Scoop waved us toward the back of the truck. "It's easy. Come inside. I show you."

"You mean I can work, too?" Willy asked.

"Sure. I need good men in here."

Willy flexed his muscles.

Uncle Scoop chuckled and handed me and Willy thin vinyl gloves, then turned on the ice machine. Within minutes, we were experts. "This is easy," I said, pouring strawberry syrup over a cone that Willy had just packed with ice.

A few minutes later

Uncle Scoop nodded toward the beach. "Here they come."

Hunger drove starving swimmers up from the beach like carpenter ants. In minutes we had our hands full. Uncle Scoop cooked up hamburgers, hot dogs, and plate lunches. Willy and I packed one shave ice after another—red, yellow, green, orange, blue, purple, and three-color rainbows.

An hour later, the crowd started to thin out.

"Whew." Uncle Scoop took off his cap and dabbed his sweating forehead with a paper napkin. "Can you two watch the truck for a minute? I need go bat'troom."

"We can do it, Uncle Scoop."

"Sure," Willy added.

Uncle Scoop took his apron off and headed over to the pavilion, where the bathrooms were. For a moment I imagined that Willy was my partner, and the Lucky Lunch was our business. I liked it.

Two boys walked up and ordered shave ice, one yellow and one red. It took us less than a minute to make them. We were pro salesmen now.

"That will be two dollars," I said, as if I'd been in the shave ice business all my life. I took their five-dollar bill and gave them three dollars back. "Thank you. Come again."

The boys raised their chins like, Yeah-sure.

"I never made change before," I said, more to myself than to Willy. It was so easy to make money with a lunch truck. Maybe when I grow up I might have one, too.

A cackling laugh snapped me out of my daydream.

"Bwahahahaha . . ." *Snort-snort.* "Bwaaahaha! Look what Uncle Scoop wen' drag up! Bwahahaha . . ." *Snort!*

"Aw, man," I mumbled.

17

Two Reds and One Blue

Tito almost choked on his own cackle.

He slapped his leg and staggered around, laughing and snorting and pointing at me and Willy. Bozo and Frankie Diamond were laughing, too, but not like somebody with a golf ball for a brain.

I glanced toward the pavilion, hoping to see Uncle Scoop coming back.

No such luck.

Tito finally got control of himself. "Hey, let's have a shave ice," he said to Bozo and Frankie Diamond. "I never had one made by midgets before."

Bozo bounced on his toes. "Yeah cool, Tito, cool. Hey you midgets, make me one blue one. Put plenny juice on top, too, ah, no cheat."

Frankie Diamond half snorted.

I didn't get Frankie Diamond. He didn't seem like a Tito-Bozo kind of guy. He didn't seem that dumb.

"I'll take a red one," Tito said. "What you like, Frankie?"

"Red."

Tito turned back to us. "Two reds and one blue, and make um good like Bozo tell."

Were they serious, or just joking around?

"Hey, Coco-cans," Tito said. "Whose birfday you was talking about back at the store?

You going buy um cake and pointy hats, or what?"

"Pointy hats!" Bozo cackled, cracking up. "Pointy hats!"

Dingbats.

"It's for Stella," Willy said. "Not that you'd know her."

Tito looked at me, his face brightening. "Stella? You mean the girl who live with you?"

Tito had met her once, and flipped over her.

I ignored him.

"Stel-lah," Tito said again, dreamily. "What day's her birfday? I might bring her something, too."

Oh, no! Stella would kill me if he showed up again. Last time, he brought her a bag of cuttlefish. She thought they were bugs. "It's Monday," I said. "But don't come over. We won't be there, we're going to . . . uh, a movie."

Tito nodded. "Monday. Good. I come then, say happy birfday, bring her something nice. She likes me, ah? Remember?" Tito flicked his eyebrows.

"Whatever," I mumbled.

"Whatchoo waiting for? Where's that shave ice?"

I turned the ice shaver on and stuck a hunk of ice on it. Willy packed the shavings into three cones that sat in a cone holder. We made two reds and one blue.

I handed them down. "Three dollars, please."

Tito gave me a squint. "What? You don't make um free for friends?"

I pointed to the price list. "One dollar each."

Tito frowned and pulled out a wad of dollar bills.

A *huge* wad of dollar bills.

My face felt suddenly hot. I could almost feel fire flaming out of my ears. Tito had all that money and he had to steal ten of my *cans*?

He peeled off three one-dollar bills and started to hand them up to me. But then he stopped and folded the money back into his fist. "Oh, look," he said, making a surprised face. "I wanted blue, like Bozo's. You made mines wrong."

I shook my head. "No, you said red."

Tito smiled. "No, I said blue."

Bozo giggled. Frankie Diamond turned away, shaking his head.

I looked at Willy, who shrugged. "Just make him another one."

No way, I thought. "You said red, Tito. Two reds and one blue, right, Willy?"

Willy shrugged again. "That's what I heard," he mumbled.

Tito stepped closer and whispered, "You don't make it right, I ain't paying you nothing, how's about that?" He stuffed the three dollars back into his pocket.

I made him another one. Blue. And while I made it, Tito nipped big hunks off his red one.

I handed Tito the blue shave ice.

Now he had one in each hand.

"Three dollars," I said again.

"Hey, Bozo. Pay um for me, ah? My hands are full."

Bozo took his own fat wad of dollar bills out. He peeled off three of them and paid Willy.

Now my face *really* got hot. All that money! "You should pay for that one, too," I said, pointing to the red one. "Since you're eating it."

Tito cocked his head, pretending he was considering my suggestion. "I don't think so, Coco-dork, because listen . . . if you make a mistake, you should pay for it yourself, right? Not the customer. You never heard of the customer is always right?"

Bozo nudged Tito with his elbow.

Tito turned.

Bozo nodded toward the pavilion.

Uncle Scoop was coming back.

"We go," Tito said.

They hurried off.

Frankie Diamond glanced once over his shoulder as I took a dollar out of my own pocket and put it in the cash drawer.

When I looked up, Tito, Bozo, and Frankie Diamond were nowhere in sight.

18

Cost of Doing Business

"How'd it go?" Uncle Scoop asked, climbing back into the lunch truck.

"Good," I said.

"Make any money?"

"Some."

Uncle Scoop put one hand on my shoulder

and the other on Willy's. "You two have quite a knack for working with people."

"Thanks," I said, trying to shake off the junk feeling of getting robbed, twice. Seemed I had a knack for that, too.

"Hey," someone said. "Mr. Scoop."

When I saw who it was, I got steamed all over again.

Frankie Diamond. Alone.

He glanced over his shoulder as he walked up.

Uncle Scoop grabbed his order pad. "What can I get for you?"

"I don't want anything. I just need to . . . to say something." He glanced over his shoulder again.

Uncle Scoop rested his arms on the counter. "What's up?"

"Well . . . see . . . a few minutes ago, you weren't here, but those two were, and I was here with two guys and we ordered three shave ice. My friend said they made his cone wrong and made them make it again."

Uncle Scoop nodded. "Okay."

"But they didn't make it wrong," Frankie went on. "They made it right . . . so my friend got two shave ice for the price of one."

"I see," Uncle Scoop said, keeping his eyes on Frankie Diamond.

Frankie pointed his chin at me. "That kid there? He paid for the second shave ice out of his own pocket."

Uncle Scoop raised his eyebrows. "Why are you telling me this, son?"

Frankie shrugged. "Because I seen that kid pay with his own money." Frankie looked at me, then back at Uncle Scoop. "I guess I just thought you should know that."

Uncle Scoop reached down to shake Frankie's hand. "You're right. Thank you for telling me."

Frankie hesitated, then reached up and shook. He left quickly.

Uncle Scoop watched him hurry away. "Now, that's something you boys won't see every day."

When Frankie got to the end of the lane he looked back once, then slipped around the corner.

Uncle Scoop took a dollar out of the cash drawer. "This is your money, not mine."

"But—"

"Call it the cost of doing business. Sometimes you lose a little money. But you did exactly the right thing, Calvin. A customer complained and you fixed it . . . but you sure didn't have to pay for it with your own money."

I looked at the dollar bill, which I needed . . . a lot. I stuffed it into my pocket. "Thanks, Uncle Scoop."

Uncle Scoop yawned. "I think I'm going to pack it in, boys. So let's see . . . how long did you work?"

I turned to Willy. "An hour?"

Willy shrugged. "I forgot to look at a clock."

Uncle Scoop waved it off. "Doesn't matter. I give you five bucks each. How's that?"

"Wow!" That was way more than I'd expected.

"Double wow!" Willy said.

Uncle Scoop gave us each a five-dollar bill from his cash drawer. "You boys come help me again sometime, huh?"

"For sure! We like to work, right, Willy?"

"Yeah. Lucky we ran into you, Uncle Scoop."

Uncle Scoop laughed. "I don't call this rat-trap Lucky Lunch for nothing."

19

Scratching Out the Numbers

Willy and I headed over to where the stream spilled its rusty water into the clean turquoise bay.

I shook my head, studying the crisp five-dollar bill Uncle Scoop had given me. "Can you believe he paid us this much?"

"We're rich!"

Willy and I slipped down a sandy hill into the shallow water. Dusty river silt puffed out around our feet as we dragged them along the bottom.

Willy pulled his five-dollar bill out of his pocket. "Here. Add this to what you have."

"No, Willy, that's yours."

"Take it. You can pay me back later."

Ho, I thought. This new kid was going to be one of my best friends ever, like Julio, Rubin, and Maya. "Thanks, Willy. Thanks a lot. But it's just a loan, okay?"

Willy nodded toward shore. "Let's go home and add it all up."

We headed back to our street, and to our fort in the jungle across from my house. It was a sand pit covered by jungle trash, and nobody but me, Willy, Julio, and Maya knew it was there. We slid down into it and lit up the candle.

I took all my coins and crumpled bills out and set them on the cardboard box we used as a table.

"Fourteen dollars and sixty-six cents."

"Ho, man, did we get rich today! Not too much more to make eighteen dollars."

"Yup."

We headed back to my house.

Willy had never seen my room before. He'd been in our kitchen, our yard, and out on the river in my red skiff. But my room was brand-new to him.

"Cool," he said. "I like it."

It wasn't much, but one wall was made of lava rocks, which you don't always see. It was full of cracks and crevices where centipedes hid when it rained. The other three walls were wood. But that wall was bug city.

"It used to be part of the garage."

"I *like* it."

"I got every kind of bug you can think of in here." I closed the door and locked it. "Plus it's private."

"How come you locked the door?"

"Girls."

"What girls?"

"Okay, one girl."

Willy scrunched his eyes. Huh?

"Trust me," I said.

He shrugged and picked up the glossy black-and-white photo of Little Johnny Coconut, my dad. Just like Stella's picture of her mom, it was autographed: *Love ya, big guy, Dad xo.*

"You look like him . . . sort of."

"He lives in Las Vegas."

"Why?"

"He and my mom split up. He's an entertainer."

"My mom said he's a big star."

"I guess."

Willy put the picture back. "So, how much more money do you need?"

I found a dull pencil and scratched out the numbers. "Three dollars and thirty-four cents."

"Well, we still have tomorrow."

I nodded. "Yeah . . . but I'm out of ideas."

We both flinched when someone pounded on the door.

Bam! Bam! Bam!

"Open up!"

The doorknob rattled.

"I know you're in there!"

Bam! Bam! Bam! Bam!

Can't Hide

"Now you see why I lock it?"

Willy stepped away from the door.

Bam! Bam! "Open up, or I might have to give you some Texas Nice!"

"What's Texas Nice?" Willy whispered.

"You don't want to know."

"Open this door!"

I sighed. "All right, all right, cool your jets."

"Who is it?" Willy whispered.

"Stella."

"Is she mad about something? What does she want?"

"To spout off. Watch."

I unlocked the door and opened it.

Stella was leaning into the door frame. She smirked, as if saying, You can't hide from me, you little ant.

"What?" I said.

"Your mom just called. She has to work an extra hour. Which means I have to make you dinner and feed your disappointing body. You have to go find Darci and bring her home . . . now. Any questions?"

"No."

Stella looked over my shoulder at Willy. "You again. Who are you, anyway?"

Willy stood frozen. "Uh . . ."

"He's Willy Wolf," I said. "He's from California."

Stella's eyebrows went up. "Well, at least

he's from someplace you wear shoes."

Willy gulped.

Stella squinted at him a moment, then turned back to me. "So what are you waiting for, honey, go find your sister."

She winked and smooched out her lips.

I closed the door and locked it. "*That* is why I lock my door."

Willy's mouth worked like a fish, as if the words inside were afraid to come out until they were safely out of Stella's range.

I laughed. "Don't worry. I got her wrapped around my little finger."

Willy ran a hand over his face. "She's scary."

"*Sssst!*" someone hissed.

We turned and looked behind us. Julio was leaning into the window screen, his hands cupped around his eyes. "Who's in there?"

"Heyyy," I said. "You're back."

"Yeah. Come out."

I inched open the door and peeked into the garage. When I was sure Stella wasn't there, we slipped out to join Julio.

Out on the road we came across two dead toads, flattened by cars and dried by the sun. I picked one up and flung it like a Frisbee. It sailed out and clattered back onto the road twenty feet ahead of us. "So, Julio, how's your day been?"

"Boring."

"Too bad. Me and Willy had a good one.

Hey, you seen Darci anywhere? I have to find her."

"Reena's house. In the yard."

I wasn't in any hurry. The longer I took to bring Darci home, the less I had to listen to Stella.

"So what was so good about today?" Julio asked.

I patted my back pocket, where one day I would have a wallet filled with money. "We got rich."

"What?"

"Rich, like money. I have to buy Stella a birthday present."

When we reached the dried toad, Julio kicked it, and it clacked farther up the street. "How rich?"

"Fourteen dollars and sixty-six cents rich."

Julio whistled.

I stopped and grabbed his arm. "Hey, you got any pop cans at your house?"

"Maybe."

"Let's go look."

Four. They were in a grocery bag in Julio's garage. Rinsed. Clean. No roaches, no ants.

"Twenty cents' worth," Julio said. "You can have them."

We headed back to Kalapawai Market to cash them in. Just before we got there I stopped. "Julio, go inside and see if Tito's there. If he's not, wave us in. If he is, tell him to have a nice day and run."

"What?"

I shoved him toward the store. "Be brave."

Weeds

The next day, Sunday, I got up around noon. Luckily, Tito hadn't been at Kalapawai, and my pile of cash had grown twenty cents higher.

I yawned and stretched. Making money sure took a lot out of you. I went into the house.

Mom was in the kitchen peeling a tangerine

for Darci. "Well," she said. "I was just about to go out and see if you were still on this planet."

I scratched my head and grabbed the orange juice from the fridge.

"Use a glass."

I found one on the counter.

"That one's dirty."

I looked into it. A curve of dried milk edged the bottom. Clean enough. I poured juice into it and gulped it down.

"When was the last time you took a shower, Cal?"

I sniffed my T-shirt.

"Not your shirt. You."

I shrugged. "Where's Darci?"

"Watching cartoons."

"Where's Stella?"

"She went to her friend Tina's house. What is this, the Inquisition?"

"What's the Inquisition?"

"Are you hungry?"

"Yeah, but Mom . . . do you have any jobs I can do to make money?"

Mom studied me. It wasn't a question I made a habit of asking. "Well, you can clean your room for a start. I shouldn't have to pay you for that, but if you do a good job I'll consider it."

Ick.

"What else?"

"Mow the lawn. Pull weeds. Clean the garage. Wash out the garbage can. Fold laundry . . . no, not that. I'll just have to do it again."

I considered my options. I sure didn't want to mow the lawn, and cleaning my room was out of the question. The garbage can was so disgusting I'd probably pass out just by taking the lid off, and the garage would take all day.

"I guess I'll pull weeds."

Mom put a fist on her

hip and looked at me. "Fine. You can start with the flower bed out front . . . but only after you eat something."

I grabbed the Frosted Mini-Wheats out of the pantry and shook the box. Scraps. I reached in for the last few. "How much will you pay me?"

"You're snacking, not eating. Get a bowl and add milk."

I got a bowl. There were seven Mini-Wheats. I poured milk on them. Mom rolled her eyes and shook her head. "Write it on my grocery list."

"So how much?"

"That depends on how much work you do and how well you do it." Mom leaned against the sink and crossed her arms. "What's this all about, anyway? I mean, this sudden desire to make money."

I didn't want to tell her, because it was supposed to be a surprise. I shrugged. "I might need it . . . someday."

Mom snorted. "Isn't *that* the truth."

Ten minutes later I was kneeling on the hard, sun-baked dirt under our front window. Mom's flowers looked like starving prisoners in a chain gang, guarded by an army of wiry weeds.

I pulled one.

It broke off. The bottom part stayed in the dirt, like it was cemented there. The stub looked up at me like, That's all you got?

"Whatcha doing, Calvin?"

I sat back on my heels. "Pulling weeds."

Darci knelt beside me. "Is it fun?"

"Sure, lots. Want to try?"

Darci nibbled her thumb. "Which one should I pull?"

"How about . . . um . . . that one."

Darci pulled. The weed broke off, just like mine.

"Fun, huh?"

"Let's do more."

Together we broke weeds and piled them

on the grass. I didn't mind this work. It was good for thinking. And what I thought of was how much I was earning and how close to eighteen dollars I was getting.

"Hey, Darce. Do you have any money you don't want? Like in your bank, or something?"

"Maybe. Do you want it?"

"To borrow, yeah. I need to buy Stella a birthday present . . . but it's a surprise, so keep it to yourself."

"A secret! I won't tell anyone." Darci jumped up. "I'll go look."

"Yeah, look," I said.

I broke off more weeds. The pile was grow-ing.

I heard a car pull up and looked over my shoulder.

It was Ledward.

Mom's boyfriend.

22

If It's Broke, Fix It

Ledward parked his World War II army jeep on the grass. He'd told me it was once an abandoned rusty old hulk covered by weeds and vines up in the jungle. "Still had a good body. The engine needed work, but with some new parts, it could run again. If it's broke, fix it, ah? That's all."

I went back to weeding.

Ledward came up and stood over me. He was so big and tall he blocked out the sun and half the sky. "Whatchoo doing down there, boy?"

"Weeding." I didn't look up.

He squatted next to me. He smelled good, like he'd just shaved or something. "Mind if I try?"

I looked at him like, Really? "Sure, go ahead."

Ledward grabbed a weed in his huge hand. He wiggled it a little, and slowly pulled it up at

an angle. The whole thing came out, roots and all. He shook dirt off and laid the weed across his huge palm. "See this? That's the roots. You don't get them out, the weed just going be poking its head up again tomorrow."

I looked at the army of broken stems I'd left in the dirt. I was going to see a whole new regiment tomorrow.

"Best thing is if you use a weeder," Ledward said. "Let me go see what I got in my jeep."

I sat back and waited. Ledward did a lot of stuff around our house. He could fix anything. If he had something to make this job easier, I was all for it.

He came back and handed me a screwdriver. "Try this."

I worked the screwdriver into the dirt, angling it under a fresh weed. I pulled, slowly, wiggling it the way Ledward had.

The weed came out . . . all of it. "Hey! It works."

Ledward tapped my shoulder. "Now you got um."

"Thanks."

"No problem. Your mama home?"

"Yeah. Inside."

Ledward stood and went into the house. He didn't knock, just walked right in. He'd been coming around to see Mom for more than a year now.

Darci came back with her life savings tucked under her arm. It was in a gray box that looked like a bank vault with a combination lock. She plopped down cross-legged on the grass and opened it up. A few coins spilled out.

"Hmm," I said, picking them up. "Twenty-seven cents. Can I borrow it?"

"Uh-huh, you want to borrow the bank, too?"

"Naah, you can keep that."

I stuck the twenty-seven cents in my pocket and pulled weeds until the sun made my back feel as if Mom was ironing my shirt with me in it.

"Enough," I finally said. "Let's go find Mom."

She was on the back patio with Ledward. They were lounging in plastic chairs and sipping tall glasses of iced tea with green mint leaves in them.

Mom raised her glass as I walked up. "There's more of this in the kitchen."

"How long did I work?"

Mom looked over her shoulder at the clock hanging on a rusty nail next to the sliding screen door. "Forty minutes."

She took a sip of tea.

Ledward gazed out over the weedy backyard. I was surprised the flimsy chair he was squeezed into could hold him up without collapsing.

But I was there for my money. "Um . . . can I get paid?"

"Well . . . let's go see how much work you did."

Darci and I followed Mom and Ledward around to the front. Mom nudged the pile of weeds with her toe. It was only about the size of someone's crumpled-up T-shirt. "Is this all you're going to do?"

I shrugged. "Yeah . . . I guess."

Mom chewed her thumbnail, thinking. "Well, how much do you think I should pay you?"

That was a question I had an answer for—about three dollars would do it. But that was too much for the meager pile of weeds drying up in the sun by her feet.

I shrugged.

Mom thought some more. "What do you think, Led?"

"He should do it for free. He lives here. He should work. Help out."

I stared at my dirty feet.

Mom nodded. "Of course, you're right. But he wanted to make some money today."

Ledward didn't say more, and I was glad about that. But I knew what he was thinking, and he was right. I hadn't done enough to get paid.

"Okay, here's the deal," Mom said. "You pick up the clothes all over the floor in your room and put them in the laundry basket, then I'll give you two dollars. How's that?"

Ho! That was way more than the nothing I should have gotten. "Deal," I said, before she could change her mind.

"And do something with that pile of weeds, too. They'll kill the grass if you just leave them there."

In my opinion the grass was so thick and healthy, not even rat poison could kill it.

I nudged Darci. "Scoop up that pile of weeds, Darce. We got some figuring to do."

We sat on the lower bunk in my room and spread what looked like a fortune out on the blanket. "Eighty-seven cents, Darce. That's all I need. Eighty-seven cents!"

"What are you getting for Stella?"

I told her about the Chris Botti CD, and how much Stella was going to love it.

"I made her a note," Darci said.

"A note?"

"Uh-huh, and I already gave it to her. It says I'll make her bed five times, for free."

I laughed. "That's good, Darce."

We found ninety-one cents in the dusty valleys of our living room couch and fifteen more under the seats in Mom's car.

"Yes!" I cheered. "Eighteen dollars and nineteen cents! I'm there, Darce! I'm *there*!"

23

Feeling Rich

I punched my alarm clock at seven the next morning.

Monday.

Stella's sixteenth birthday.

I jumped down from the top bunk and pulled on my jeans. I counted the extra nineteen cents out of my fortune and set it aside to pay Darci back. Eighteen dollars went into my pocket. A few bills and a lot of coins. It made a big bulge, and was as heavy as a fistful of nails. I patted it, feeling richer than I'd ever been in my life. Too bad by tonight I'd be broke again. In debt, too. I also had to pay Willy back.

In the kitchen, Mom and Stella were making lunches as usual. I grabbed the orange juice out of the fridge and started to drink from the spout.

"Stop!" Mom said, scowling at me. "Why is it that you can't hold even the tiniest thought in your head? How many times have I told you not to drink from the carton?"

"Sorry."

I got a glass.

Stella eyed me. "What you got in your pocket, Stump?"

"Mom! She called me Stump again."

"Be nice, Stella," Mom said. "He's impressionable. We don't want to diminish his self-esteem."

"He's got self-esteem?"

"Calvin, is there something you want to say to Stella this morning?"

I looked at Mom. Huh?

Mom sighed. "What *day* is this?"

"Uh, Monday?"

Mom squinted at me. "Happy birthday, Stella," she said, scolding me with her eyes.

"Oh. Yeah. Uh . . . happy birthday."

Stella pinched my cheek. "Thank you for remembering, Stumpy. That's sweet of you."

I was *so* glad my room was way out in the garage. I couldn't even imagine living as close to Stella as Darci did.

In the pantry I found a brand-new box of Honey Nut Cheerios. I got a bowl and took it to the counter. Darci wandered in and climbed up onto the stool next to me.

Stella thunked a carton of milk down between us.

"Five minutes," Mom said, leaving the kitchen. "I'm driving you to school today." Sometimes we walked.

I ate and left my bowl where it was on the

counter. By the time I got home from school that afternoon, it would be crawling with ants. Maybe there'd even be a dead fly in it. Which would be great. I could feed it to Manly Stanley.

I grabbed my backpack and stuffed my lunch into it.

"Hey!" Stella snapped. "You can't just leave your bowl there for the ants to crawl into while you're pretending to learn something in school. Take it to the sink and rinse it out."

Tell me again why I went through all that trouble to make eighteen dollars?

24

Chris Botti

After school Willy, Julio, Rubin, and Maya waited for me at the jungle gym while I got Darci. We were all going to the music store to turn my cash into a Chris Botti CD.

"Let's go," I said, running up.

Julio pointed with his chin. "Look."

Tito, Bozo, and Frankie Diamond had a

couple of third graders surrounded. Robbery in progress. Time to slip away unseen.

"Run silent, run fast," I said.

At the music store, we crowded around the jazz section.

I snapped up the brand-new Chris Botti CD. "This is it."

Darci, Maya, Julio, Willy, and Rubin pushed in to see.

"Is he a singer, or what?" Maya asked.

I shrugged. "Don't ask me."

Keoni the sales guy was at the counter. "You're back."

Darci and Maya gawked at the two rings poking through his lower lip.

I dumped the wad of money on the counter.

"Ho! You rob a parking meter or something?"

"Worked for it," I said, feeling proud that I'd made most of the money myself.

Keoni shook his head and scanned the

137

price code, then set the CD on the counter. "Eighteen dollars and seventy-two cents."

I gaped at him. What?

Keoni leaned down on the counter. "You want me to help you count it out?"

"But . . ."

I looked down at the pile of money. "I . . . I thought it was eighteen dollars."

Keoni rescanned the CD. "Yep, eighteen."

"But you just said eighteen dollars and . . . something."

"Well, with tax it's eighteen seventy-two."

"Tax?"

"Tax . . . you know what that is?"

"No."

After all the work and scrambling I'd done, I *still* didn't have enough money? I stared at the pile of coins and bills.

"Listen," Keoni said. "Let's just see what we've got here."

Keoni separated the bills and coins into neat piles and counted it all up. "Eighteen dollars, right on the nose." He leaned forward and cupped his chin in his hand. "You're short seventy-two cents. You got that in your pocket?"

I shook my head. I felt like I'd been slapped in the face with a wet T-shirt. "No," I mumbled. "That's everything."

I stared at all the money. It looked like a lot. "I guess I can't buy it."

Keoni nodded.

The Chris Botti CD lay on the counter, shiny new in its plastic wrap. "It was a birthday present," I whispered.

A silent moment passed.

"Tell you what," Keoni said. He dug into his pocket. "If I have seventy-two cents, you can have it."

"Really?"

Keoni smiled. "I think you might be in luck." He poured a handful of pennies, nickels, and dimes onto the counter. He had the seventy-two cents and added it to the pile. "How did you get all this money, anyway?"

"Me and my friends collected cans and made shave ice and pulled weeds and found some money in the couch and the car."

Keoni snorted. "Sounds like how my dad got this store. He scratched up every last buck he could find."

"This is your dad's store?"

"Every spider-infested corner of it."

"Wow."

Keoni bagged the CD and walked us to the door. "You folks come back again, okay?"

"We will," we all said, heading out into the sun. "Thank you, mister, thank you!"

At Maya's house, we found some wrapping paper that was shiny pink with little red hearts all over it. It was in the laundry room, left over from Valentine's Day.

"Is this all you have?" I asked.

Maya shrugged. "Sorry."

"Fine."

I wrapped the Chris Botti CD. Darci helped me make a birthday card using red, blue, green, and yellow markers.

I signed the bottom: *From Calvin Coconut*.

Darci signed: *Love, Darci*.

"You sign, too," I said, handing Willy the pen. "You made a lot of the money to buy this."

Willy put up his hands. "No, no. This is your present."

I looked at my friends. They'd all helped out.

Maya grinned. "Think she'll like it?"

That was a good question.

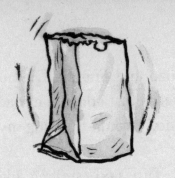

25

Tito Meets Clarence

Later that afternoon, Tito kept his word.

I was in my garage-bedroom scribbling down how much I owed Willy and Darci when I saw movement in the window and looked up.

Tito was standing in our driveway with a brown paper grocery bag. Across the street I could see Bozo and Frankie Diamond squatting in the weeds that edged the road.

"No, no, no," I said, dropping my pencil.

I ran out.

"Heyyy," Tito said, smiling like he was glad to see me. "Coco-pal, howzit?"

"What are you *doing* here? You got to go!"

"Is that any way to treat a friend? Come on, bro, be nice."

I frowned and looked over my shoulder at the front window. Stella was home, and if she saw Tito she'd—

Tito raised the paper bag. "I just want to give Stella something . . . for her birfday."

"What is it?"

"Surprise . . . for Stella, ah? Not you." Tito grinned.

I frowned and looked across the street. Frankie Diamond waved. Bozo gave me stink eye.

This is bad, I thought. Bad, bad, bad.

Tito started for the front door.

I tried to block him, but he shoved me aside. "I said be nice, Coco-punk, or else I might have to rearrange your face. You like I do that?"

I winced when I saw Stella squinting out the window.

Tito saw her, too, and blew her a kiss.

Jeese!

Stella banged out the door before Tito took another step. She blocked his way, her hands on her hips. "Rag boy," she said.

Rag boy. The one other time Stella had seen Tito he was wearing a T-shirt with stains all over it. She said, "You always wear rags?" It was funny . . . then.

Tito must have thought rag boy was one of Stella's terms of endearment, because he didn't even blink.

"Heyyy," he said, grinning like a horse.

Stella glowered over Tito's shoulder, giving

me a look that made Bozo's stink eye look like a Valentine's card.

I shrugged. What could I do?

Then I heard a familiar sound in the distance. I turned to look down the street.

Boooom . . . boooom . . . boooom.

Tito heard it, too, and nodded his head to the beat, playing it cool. He lifted the grocery bag toward Stella. "I brought you a birfday present."

Stella gave him a long stare. "*Birf*day?"

"Yeah." He winked. "Happy birfday . . . Stel-lah."

Good grief.

Stella eyed the bag.

Boooom . . . boooom . . . boooom.

Across the street Bozo and Frankie Diamond sprang to their feet, their eyes glued to the big pink car rumbling closer.

Tito jiggled the grocery bag.

Stella didn't take it. "What's in it?"

"A present. I got um for you at the store. Some kids had a box of them. I got it free."

Stella hesitated, then took the bag.

The pink car thumped closer.

Boooom . . . boooom . . . boo—

The radio went off as Clarence pulled up and parked his pink supertanker in our driveway.

Stella peeked into the bag.

"Yahhh!" she shrieked. *"Yahhhhhhhhhhhhh!"*

Clarence stumbled out of the car and ran over. He grabbed the bag from Stella. Stella ran back into the house, the screen door slapping and echoing down the river.

Tito stood frozen, confused, gaping.

I gaped, too, wondering what the spit was in that bag.

Clarence peeked in, then looked up at Tito.

Tito blinked.

Clarence reached gently into the brown paper grocery bag and came out with a fluffy white kitten, so small it fit into his hand like a parakeet. He scratched the kitten's chin, his eyes still on Tito. "Who you, boy?"

"Uh . . . me . . . uh . . . uh . . . I go Calvin's

147

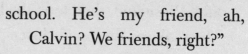

school. He's my friend, ah, Calvin? We friends, right?"

I nodded. "Sure, uh . . . yeah." It was that or get strangled next time I see Tito.

Clarence turned toward the house. Stella stood in the front window looking out, holding a dishrag over her nose and mouth.

"Stella," Clarence said, turning back to Tito. "She's allergic to cats."

"Oh."

Clarence studied Tito, petting the white kitten.

Tito cleared his throat. "Well . . . I go now." He looked at the kitten. "What I going do with that?"

"I take it," Clarence said. "Give it to my sister."

"Yeah-yeah, good, give um your sister, good." Tito backed away. He nodded to me once to remind Clarence we really were good friends, and when he reached Bozo and Frankie Diamond in the weeds, they took off like spooked mongooses.

Clarence nodded to me. Hey.

Hey, I nodded back.

"You got a small box I can use?"

"I'll go see." I ran into the garage. There was an old shoe box. "This okay?"

"Perfect."

Clarence took the box and gently set the kitten in it.

He handed the box to me. "Hold this a minute, ah? I got something for Stella in the car."

I took the shoe box, careful not to touch the kitten. If any cat got on me, Stella might swell up again. Luckily, the kitten curled up and went to sleep.

Clarence stopped by the spigot on the side of the house. Water gushed out and splashed his feet. He squatted on his heels and washed his hands, over and over. When he was done, he stood and wiped them on his shorts.

When he saw me watching, he flicked his eyebrows. "Cat."

I nodded.

Clarence headed for his car and brought out a bunch of flowers and six papayas, the best I'd ever seen.

He gave them to Stella, then drove away.

Boooom . . . boooom . . . boooom.

Hearts

That night we celebrated Stella's birthday.

Mom cooked up Stella's favorite dinner and invited Ledward and Clarence over. Clarence couldn't come because he had to take his little sister to hula class.

But Ledward came, and the minute he walked into the house, Mom grabbed his arm and steered him into the kitchen. I was sticking candles into the cake Mom had brought home that said HAPPY SWEET SIXTEEN.

Mom pushed a wrapped gift into Ledward's hands. "This is for Stella. It's from you."

Ledward took the present and played along.

"And this one is from me," Mom said, handing him another one. "Would you take them out and put them next to her plate on the table?"

Mom had tied white helium balloons to Stella's chair, and though Stella tried to look embarrassed when we all sat down, I could tell that she really didn't mind. She even smiled.

Mom and Ledward sat at opposite ends of the table. Darci and I sat in the middle, across from Stella.

Mom took some spaghetti and passed the bowl around. "Did your mom call you this afternoon, Stella?"

Stella hesitated. "No . . . not yet."

"Well, maybe she'll call tonight."

Stella nodded. "Maybe."

Maybe not, I thought. When Stella first moved in with us Mom said Stella and her mom needed a break from each other. They never seemed to call each other.

Ledward spun spaghetti onto his fork. "When I was sixteen, I moved furniture. Hardest work I ever did."

Stella said nothing.

Ledward took a bite, chuckling, thinking back. "Every birthday I ever had, my moms made me a coconut cake. Nowadays, I still love coconut cake."

Mom smiled. "Well, then, you'd fit right in here at the Coconut home."

"I like that thought."

What?

Ledward looked at Mom, shylike. "I mean—"

"So," Mom said, turning to Stella. "How does it feel to be sixteen?"

Stella shrugged. "I can get a driver's license."

"You sure can," Mom said.

For a moment nobody spoke.

We finished eating.

Mom reached over and tapped my hand. "Grab some of these plates and come with me."

I followed her into the kitchen and set the plates by the sink. Mom handed me a book of matches. "Light them up."

We sang "Happy Birthday," the candle glow wobbling on Stella's face. When she blew out the candles, I watched to see that she didn't spit all over the cake.

Mom nodded toward Stella's gifts. "Looks like you got a couple of presents. I wonder who they're from?"

Stella reached for one and tore off the wrapping paper. "Thank you!" she said, lifting the gold necklace Mom had gotten her out of its long box. "It's beautiful!"

Mom beamed. "It will look great on you."

Stella put it on. "I love it."

Darci pushed the other present toward Stella. "This one's from Ledward."

Stella opened it and looked up.

"Uh—uh," Ledward stammered. "That's uh . . . that's uh . . . a book about . . . uh."

"It's a book about her life," Mom said smoothly. "One she will write herself. What a nice thought, Ledward. Every girl needs a journal."

"Yeah," Ledward said. "You write it."

Stella eyed Ledward like, Right. "Thank you," she said.

"No problem."

Mom turned to me. "Calvin, did you get something for Stella, too?" Her frozen smile said, You're toast if you didn't.

"Me and Darci got her one together."

"*Darci and I* got her one," Mom said.

"You and Darci got her one, too?" I said.

"Let's just see what you have, Calvin."

It was on the floor under my chair. I picked it up and gave it to Stella. She read the card, smiled, and showed it to Mom.

Mom beamed. "This is so *sweet*."

Stella reached across the table and touched Darci's hand. "It's a really nice card, Darci. You made it, right?"

"Calvin did some of it, too."

Stella took the card back and squinted at it. "Oh . . . yeah . . . I see he signed it."

"Hardy-har."

Stella picked up the birthday present

wrapped in Valentine's Day paper. She looked at me. "Hearts?"

I shrugged.

"Love must be in the air," Ledward said, and winked.

"Not!" I spat.

"Ledward," Mom said.

He held up his hands, grinning.

Mom turned back to Stella. "What did Calvin give you?"

"It's from Darci, too," I muttered.

Stella unwrapped it, slowly at first. But when she got a glimpse of what was inside, she ripped the paper away, grabbed the CD, and raised it above her head. "Yes!"

Mom looked at me, then back at Stella. "What is it?"

"The new Chris Botti CD! The one I wanted!"

Mom turned back to me, confused. "How did—"

"The weeds . . . and some other stuff."

Mom's eyes flooded. "Oh, Calvin."

Stella hugged Chris Botti. She looked at him again, and kissed him.

It was starting to freak me out. I turned to Ledward.

Ledward pushed his chair back. "Uh . . . how's about you and me go do the dishes."

27

New Stella

The next morning in the kitchen Stella lurked over me as I took my time with a bowl of crunchy Grape-Nuts.

"Tell me the truth," she whispered. "Your mom bought that CD for you to give to me. I mean, you didn't actually think of it yourself, right?"

"I thought of it. I saw your poster and—"

"You went into my *room*?"

"Uh . . . when I woke you up I saw it."

Stella eyed me.

"I bought it with my own money, too," I added.

"What money?"

"I had some."

Stella pinched her jaw, still looking at me.

"What?" I said.

"I'm trying to figure out if you're telling the truth."

"Do I look like I would lie?"

Stella laughed. "Cute comeback."

"So how'd she like it?" Willy asked at school.

"She thinks my mom bought it for me to give to her."

Willy frowned. "Well, that stinks."

That evening after an early dinner Mom told Darci and me to brush our teeth, then she sat on the couch with a magazine and the pillow from her bed.

I nudged Darci. "Watch. She'll be asleep in five minutes."

We squeezed toothpaste onto our toothbrushes and crowded around the bathroom sink. Stella appeared in the mirror, leaning against the doorframe with her arms crossed.

I stopped brushing, and with foamy white toothpaste bubbling over my lips, garbled, "Wha–do–you–ont?"

"You and Darci want to hear something?"

I spat and dipped my head under the tap. "What is it?"

"Come to my room when you're done."

Stella left.

Darci and I glanced at each other. I spun circles around my ear with my finger. Darci giggled.

We crept down the hall to Stella's room. The door was open. Stella was lying across her bed with her feet on the wall, staring up at Chris Botti. Clarence's flowers were in a vase on the windowsill. They glowed against the dusky sky.

"You can come in," she said, without even looking to see that we were there. "Sit. Better yet, lie down."

Darci and I sprawled on the floor. This is weird, I thought.

Stella rolled off her bed and went over to her CD player. Music came on. "This is Chris Botti."

We listened. The music was nice. Peaceful.

"When's he going to sing?" I asked.

"He's a trumpet player, not a singer."

"Oh."

The music made me sleepy. But I liked the clean sound of Chris Botti's trumpet. It made me think of the ocean.

"It makes me want to cry," Stella whispered.

I looked up. "Why?"

"I don't know."

We listened.

When Stella saw that Darci had fallen

asleep, she sighed and knelt to lift her up and carry her to her room. She stopped and looked down at me. "I know your mom didn't buy this CD for you to give to me."

"You do?"

"She told me."

This was so strange. Stella was talking like a nice person, and not calling me names. I hoped she would never-ever-ever hear anything about Zippy and her pillow. That was over. Gone. Done.

Chris Botti played on.

"You can listen to the whole thing if you want."

I did.

In fact, I almost fell asleep, too.

Sometime later, Stella nudged me with her foot. "I didn't say you could sleep in here, honey."

28

Kitty, Kitty

I got up and stumbled out to my room.

Hatchet lay where I'd tossed it on my lower bunk. I grabbed it and looked out the window. The dark mountains were sharp against the glow of the sun setting on the other side of the island. Maybe a half hour of sunlight left.

I took the book outside and sat on the

grass. Something moving in the weeds across the street caught my eye. It was black, and fat. Aw, man.

"Git!" I hissed. "Go home!"

Zippy slouched out of the weeds, ignoring me.

I shook my head and went back to *Hatchet.*

This is so strange, I thought. Stella picked this book out for me. Not only that, from the way Mom made it sound, she'd actually put some thought into choosing it, too.

I stared at the cover. Smelled the new pages.

What a crazy few days: the watermelon dress, me and Zippy ruining Stella's date with Clarence, collecting cans, getting robbed, making shave ice, Chris Botti's red hearts, and Tito's kitten. Man oh man.

I remembered what Ledward had said about his old jeep, too: *If it's broke, fix it. That's all.*

I opened *Hatchet* and started reading.

It was good. I liked it.

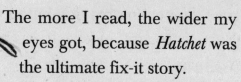

The more I read, the wider my eyes got, because *Hatchet* was the ultimate fix-it story.

I looked up and smiled when I realized that something was missing—the crummy feeling.

I yawned.

Then nearly fell over when I saw that Zippy had sneaked past me and was cruising toward the house.

I scrambled up. "Scat! Get out of here!"

Zippy took off, heading toward the back of the house.

"Zippy, stop! Here kitty, kitty!"

He scooted around the corner.

"Come back here!"

I found him crouching in the weeds . . . right under Stella's open window.

"Zippy," I whispered.

I crouched, too, and tried to be still, to stop scaring him. Chris Botti drifted smoothly out the window.

"It's me, Zippy. Remember?

The one who always saves you? You owe me, Zip. Come here."

Zippy eyed me.

I inched closer and scooped him up, then sprinted to the front of the house. I dumped him in the weeds across the street. "Go home! Git!"

Zippy headed into the bushes.

Thirty seconds later he swaggered back out and plopped down in the middle of the road.

"Come on, Zip," I pleaded. "Give me a break."

I promise, this really happened: Zippy grinned at me.

True fact.

A Hawaii Fact:

Hawaii's state fish is the reef triggerfish, or *Rhinecanthus rectangulus*. But in Hawaii we call it by its real name: humuhumunukunukuapua'a.

A Calvin Fact:

A cockroach can live for weeks with its head cut off. After a while, it dies of starvation.